Aesop is thought to be the author
of more than two hundred fables. Fables are short
tales, usually about talking animals, that teach
lessons about right and wrong. Very little
is known about Aesop, but some scholars
think he lived in Greece more than
two thousand years ago, about 600 BC,
and may have been a slave who was freed
by his master.

Retold by Ronne Randall
Edited by Juli Barbato
Illustrated by David Frankland
Line illustrations by John Lawrence

Cover illustration by James Bernardin

Originally published in the United Kingdom by
Ladybird Books Ltd © 1994

First American edition by Ladybird Books USA
An Imprint of Penguin USA Inc.
375 Hudson Street, New York, New York 10014

Printed in Great Britain
10 9 8 7 6 5 4 3 2 1
ISBN 0-7214-5651-0

PICTURE CLASSICS

AESOP'S FABLES

Contents

Contents

In his loudest voice, the boy cried, "Wolf! Wolf!"

THE BOY WHO CRIED "WOLF!"

Once there was a boy who looked after his father's flock of sheep. Every day he took the sheep to graze on the hillside and stayed with them until sundown.

The boy did not like being on his own all day and grew very bored with his job. One day he had an idea. "I will cry 'Wolf! Wolf!'" he thought. "Then people from the village will run up to help me. It will be fun to see their faces when they find that there isn't a wolf here after all!"

So the boy stood up and, in his loudest voice, cried, "Wolf! Wolf!" Sure enough, several people rushed up the hill to help him.

The boy greeted them all with a big grin. "There isn't a wolf," he said. "It was just a joke! Ha, ha, ha!"

The people didn't laugh. They were annoyed and grumbled all the way back to the village. But the boy was very pleased with himself.

The next day, the boy cried "Wolf! Wolf!" again. This time the people who came to help were even angrier than before. When it happened a third time, they were positively fed up.

Then one day a wolf really did come. "Wolf! Wolf!" the boy shouted at the top of his voice.

The villagers didn't even bother to look up. "That boy is up to his old tricks again," they muttered, and went about their work.

With no one to help him, the boy could not fight off the wolf, and it killed the entire flock.

MORAL: *If you tell lies, no one will believe you when you tell the truth.*

THE ROOSTERS
AND THE EAGLE

Once upon a time, there were two roosters who lived in the same farmyard. Each rooster thought he was better than the other and should be master of the yard. They spent nearly every day arguing with each other.

At last the roosters decided that the only way to settle the matter was to have a fight. The winner would then be master of the farmyard.

The morning of the fight came. As the other farm animals watched, the roosters charged at each other, striking with their claws and pecking at each other mercilessly.

At last one of them was beaten. With his tail drooping and his feathers broken and spattered with blood, he crept off to a corner of the farmyard to nurse his wounds.

The other rooster was filled with pride at his

victory. Puffing up his feathers, he flew to the top of the fence and crowed triumphantly: *"Cock-a-doodle-doo! Cock-a-doodle-doo!"*

The crowing caught the attention of an eagle who was hunting nearby.

"That sounds like a good, strong bird," the eagle said to himself. "I'll bet he's tasty, too!"

The eagle flew straight to the farmyard, swooped down, and caught the proud rooster in his talons. The rooster made an excellent dinner for the eagle.

With his rival gone, the first rooster came out of his corner and took his place on top of the fence. No one could deny that he was now master of the farmyard!

MORAL: *Pride can lead to a downfall.*

The eagle swooped down

BELLING THE CAT

Once there were some mice who lived in a house. They had a cozy little home behind a wall, and the scraps they found to eat were always delicious.

There was only one thing to spoil their happiness. A big cat lived in the house, too. Every day, the cat caught a mouse and ate it.

At last the mice said to one another, "We must do something about that cat. If she isn't stopped soon, she will eat us all!"

So all the mice tried to come up with a way to stop the cat from eating them. After a while, one old mouse said, "I've thought of something. If we put a bell on the cat, we'll always hear her coming. Then, we can run away and hide."

"What a good idea!" said the other mice. So they scurried off to look for a bell. As soon as they found one, they took it to the old mouse. "It was your idea," they said, "so you should bell the cat."

"Oh, no!" said the old mouse. "I am much too old. I can't run as fast as you younger mice. One of you should do it!"

"*We* can't do it," said the younger mice. "What would happen to our poor families if one of us got hurt?"

"And *we* can't do it," said the baby mice. "We're much too little!"

In the end, no one would agree to put the bell on the cat. So the cat continued to eat the mice, until they were all gone.

MORAL: *Some things are more easily said than done.*

The grapes were too high for the fox

THE FOX AND THE GRAPES

A fox was walking through the countryside one afternoon when he passed a house with a grapevine growing next to it. From the vine hung big bunches of fat, juicy grapes.

The fox was hungry, and he wanted some of those grapes. So he hurried over to the grapevine.

But the grapes were too high for the fox. No matter how high he jumped, he could not reach them.

At last the fox gave up. "Those grapes are probably sour, anyway," he said to himself as he walked away. He knew it wasn't true — but he wanted to believe it!

MORAL: *It is easy to say you don't want the things you cannot have.*

THE TORTOISE AND THE HARE

One day, a hare was bragging to his friends about how fast he could run. "I am swifter than any animal in this forest," he said. "I challenge anyone to beat me in a race!"

The other animals were fed up with the hare's boasting, but none of them was brave enough to accept his challenge.

None of them, that is, except for an old tortoise.

"I will race you," said the tortoise, slowly making his way up to the hare.

"You?" laughed the hare. "You're so slow you can hardly walk, much less run! No, it wouldn't be a fair contest — it would be much too easy for me!"

"Nevertheless," the tortoise insisted, "I would like to try."

"All right," said the hare. "We'll race from here to the stream on the other side of the clearing."

The other animals gathered to watch. Some of them ran ahead to the stream, so they could see the winner cross the finish line.

"Ready, set, go!" cawed the crow from its perch in a treetop.

Off went the hare, as quick as a flash. The tortoise set out slowly, one step at a time.

When he reached the clearing, the hare looked back. The tortoise was nowhere to be seen.

"He's so far behind, it will take him ages to catch up with me," the hare said to himself. "I may as well have a rest!" And he curled up next to a tree stump and went to sleep.

Meanwhile, the tortoise kept walking, slowly and steadily, one step at a time. Soon he came to the tree stump where the hare was sleeping. He smiled to himself and kept walking.

Hours later, the hare woke up. "I'd better finish the race!" he thought. He looked around and laughed when he couldn't see the tortoise anywhere.

"He *still* hasn't caught up with me!" the hare chuckled.

But as the hare ran to the stream, there was the tortoise, just crossing the finish line! All the animals were cheering. The tortoise won the race!

It was a long time before the animals heard the hare boasting again.

MORAL: *Slow and steady wins the race.*

The tortoise won the race!

THE ANT AND
THE DOVE

In a forest one day, a thirsty ant went to a stream to get a drink. But he slipped on the muddy bank and fell into the water. The ant did not know how to swim, so he could not get out of the stream.

A dove who was flying by happened to look down and see the ant struggling. "That little ant is in danger," she thought. "I must help him!"

She flew off to the nearest tree and plucked a big leaf, which she dropped down to the ant.

The grateful ant climbed onto the leaf. On this little raft, he drifted safely back to the bank.

Once he was on dry land again, the ant looked up at the dove. "Thank you for saving me!" he called. "I will help you some day."

A few days later, the ant was hurrying through the woods when he saw the dove sitting in a tree. Just behind her, he saw a hunter creeping up with his bow and arrow, getting ready to shoot.

"I can't let that hunter hurt my friend!" thought the ant. As quick as lightning, the ant ran over to the hunter and bit him on the leg.

"Ouch!" cried the hunter, dropping his bow and grabbing his leg. The dove, alerted by the noise, flew off to safety. As soon as she looked down and saw the hunter and the ant, she realized what had happened.

"Thank you, friend," the dove cooed down to the ant. "You did help me after all!"

MORAL: *One good turn deserves another.*

"That bone looks even tastier than mine!"

THE DOG AND
THE BONE

One day, a dog was passing a butcher's shop and saw a big, juicy bone in the window. Just looking at it made the dog's mouth water. As soon as the butcher's back was turned, the dog crept in and stole the bone. Off he ran with it, before anyone could catch him.

Carrying the bone in his mouth, the dog ran out of the village and into the countryside. He wanted to find a peaceful spot, where he could enjoy the bone without being disturbed.

Soon the dog came to a river. As he trotted along the bank, he happened to look at the water. To his surprise, he saw another dog with a big, juicy bone!

"That bone looks even tastier than mine!" thought the greedy dog. "Why shouldn't I have it? I will jump into the river and grab it."

So in he jumped. But when he was in the water, he could not find the dog, or its bone. And his own bone fell out of his mouth and sank to the bottom of the river.

As the dog climbed back onto the river bank, he looked into the water again. This time, he saw a wet, bedraggled dog—and he realized that he was looking at his own reflection.

"If I hadn't been so greedy," thought the dog, "I wouldn't have lost that big, juicy bone. Now I have nothing at all!"

MORAL: *Be content with what you have.*

THE ANT AND THE GRASSHOPPER

One warm summer's day, a grasshopper was sitting on a leaf, singing happily in the sunshine. As he sang, he happened to look down and see an ant hurrying by. The ant was carrying a large seed and seemed to be working very hard.

"Friend Ant," called the grasshopper, "why are you working so hard on such a beautiful day? You should be relaxing and enjoying the sunshine, as I am!"

"Oh, I have no time to relax," replied the ant. "I have to collect food and store it for winter. Good-bye!" And off she went with her seed.

For the rest of the summer, the grasshopper enjoyed himself. He basked in the sunshine every morning and sang every afternoon. Every day he watched the ant and her friends gathering food and carrying it back to their nest.

"You should be preparing for winter, too!" the ant

warned the grasshopper.

But the grasshopper wouldn't listen. "I'm having far too good a time, and winter's such a long way off," he said. "Why should I trouble myself?"

Time passed, and summer ended. The days grew shorter and colder, and the leaves fell from the trees. The grasshopper could no longer sit in the sunshine and sing. When he looked for food, he could find none. He was cold and hungry.

One day, when the ground was covered with snow, the grasshopper struggled to find his way to the ant's nest. She and her friends were snug and warm inside, and they were well fed.

"Please help me," begged the grasshopper. "I'm so cold and so hungry!"

"You should have gathered food when you could, as we did," said the ant. "What did you do all summer, while we were working?"

"I sang in the sunshine," said the grasshopper.

"Well," said the ant, "if you had spent some time

"What did you do all summer?"

preparing for the winter, perhaps you would not be cold and hungry now. But if you sing all summer, then you must starve all winter. I'm very sorry," she went on, "but we have only enough to feed ourselves. I'm afraid we have no food to spare for you."

So the hungry grasshopper went back out into the snow with nothing to eat.

THE RAVEN AND
THE JUG

One hot, dry summer's day, a thirsty raven flew over the parched countryside, looking for something to drink. At last she found an old, cracked jug with just a little water in it.

The jug was deep, and the raven could not reach the water. She tried to knock the jug over, she tried to move it, she even tried to break it in order to get at the water. But nothing worked.

At last the clever raven had an idea. She flew off and gathered as many little stones as she could. Then she dropped them, one by one, into the jug.

With each pebble, the water rose a little higher. At last it reached the top, and the raven had a nice, refreshing drink.

MORAL: *Necessity is the mother of invention.*

"I didn't even know you were there!"

THE GNAT AND THE BULL

One morning, a bull was grazing peacefully in a field of clover. Nearby, a gnat buzzed busily for several hours.

At last, the gnat grew tired and looked for a place to rest. He landed on one of the bull's horns. The bull kept grazing contentedly, enjoying the sweet clover.

After a while, the gnat felt rested and ready to go. "Excuse me," he called down to the bull, "but do you mind if I leave now?"

The bull looked up in surprise. "Mind?" he said. "Why should I mind? I didn't even know you were there! I didn't notice you when you arrived, and I won't notice when you go." And he went on chewing the clover.

> **MORAL:** *We are not always as important to others as we seem to ourselves.*

THE FOX
AND THE LIONESS

A mother fox and a lioness were sitting and talking one day. Eventually the conversation came around to children.

"My cubs are growing so fast!" said the mother fox. "You should see how much they eat!"

"Yes," said the lioness. "My cub is growing quickly, too."

"And how clever my cubs are!" said the mother fox. "They're already learning to hunt."

"Yes," said the lioness. "My cub is clever, too."

"I've got a litter of five beautiful cubs, you know," said the mother fox smugly. "I've noticed that you never have more than one."

"Yes," said the lioness quietly, "but that one is a lion!"

MORAL: *Quality is more important than quantity.*

THE LION
AND THE MOUSE

One day, a large, powerful lion lay sleeping peacefully in the sun. Not far away, a little mouse was scurrying home with a stalk of grain in his mouth.

The mouse was in such a hurry that he didn't watch where he was going, and he ran right over the lion's paw.

The lion woke up in a terrible rage. "How dare you disturb my sleep!" he roared, grabbing hold of the little mouse.

"I'm very sorry," squeaked the mouse, trembling with fear. "It was an accident. I'll never do it again, I promise!"

"I'll make certain of that!" said the lion, opening his mouth wide.

"Oh, please don't eat me!" begged the mouse.

"Why shouldn't I?" asked the lion.

The mouse ran to the lion at once

"Because one day," said the mouse, "I will be able to help you!"

"What?" roared the lion, bursting into laughter. "How could a tiny, weak creature like you help a mighty lion like me?"

"Let me go, and you'll see," said the mouse.

"All right," said the lion. "You wouldn't have made much of a meal, anyway." And he let the mouse go.

The very next day, the lion was walking through the forest and got caught in a hunter's trap. A net fell over him, and he could not escape. The harder he struggled, the more tangled up in the net he became. The lion roared with pain and anger.

Far away in his nest, the mouse heard the lion's roars. He ran to the lion at once.

When the mouse saw what had happened, he didn't say a word. He just climbed on the lion's back and began chewing the net.

Before long, the mouse had chewed a big hole in the net, and soon the lion was able to free himself.

As the lion climbed out of the trap, he looked directly at the mouse. "Thank you for saving my life," he said gently.

"And thank you for sparing *my* life," said the mouse. "I told you I would be able to help you, and I have kept my word."

"You have indeed!" agreed the lion.

MORAL: *Friends come in all shapes and sizes.*

THE OWL AND THE GRASSHOPPER

Once there was an owl who lived in the hollow of a big tree. Like all owls, she preferred to sleep in the daytime and hunt for food at night.

On a lower branch in the same tree, a grasshopper made his home. This grasshopper slept all night and spent his days chirping and singing very loudly.

With all the racket the grasshopper made, the owl could never get a decent day's sleep. This made her furious—until she figured out a way to stop the grasshopper's noise-making once and for all.

One day, as the grasshopper was chirping, the owl called down to him, "Dear neighbor, although your chirping keeps me awake, I don't mind at all. The music you make is so lilting and melodious that I would hate to miss it. You must be the greatest musician in the forest!"

"Oh, thank you," said the grasshopper, thrilled at

the owl's flattering words.

"In fact," the owl went on, "your music is so beautiful that it's put me in the mood for a celebration. I have some delicious, sweet nectar that I have been saving for a special occasion. Won't you come in and share it with me?"

The grasshopper's mouth watered at the thought of the tempting drink. "Thank you, kind owl," he said. "I'll be right there." And he dashed up to the hollow.

As soon as the grasshopper set foot in the owl's home, she pounced on him and gobbled him up. She slept peacefully from that day on!

MORAL: *Don't be deceived by flattery.*

"Won't you come in?"

THE GOOSE THAT LAID GOLDEN EGGS

Once upon a time, a man and his wife had a wonderful goose. Every day, it laid an egg made of pure gold.

The man and the woman were able to sell the goose's eggs for a great deal of money, and they soon grew rich. But the more they had, the more they wanted.

They tried feeding the goose extra corn to see if she might lay more than one egg a day. They bought more geese, hoping that these might lay golden eggs, too.

But nothing changed. Their goose was the only one of her kind, and despite everything they tried, she continued to lay just one golden egg a day.

One morning, the man had an idea. "If our goose lays golden eggs," he said to his wife, "then her insides must be made of gold. Let's cut her open and get all the gold out at once. That way, we can make lots of money without waiting!"

So they killed the goose and cut her open. To their surprise, they found that her insides were just like those of any other goose — they weren't made of gold at all.

Of course, now that the goose was dead, there were no more golden eggs. So the man and his wife were left with nothing.

MORAL: *Greed can make people lose everything.*

The stork couldn't eat anything at all

THE FOX AND
THE STORK

One day, a fox invited a stork to dine at his home. "Thank you," said the stork. "I would love to come."

The stork arrived, hungry and eager for dinner. "Make yourself at home," said the fox. "I'll just go and get the food."

The stork could hardly wait — wonderful smells were coming from the fox's kitchen.

But when the fox returned, the stork was filled with dismay. For the fox had served all the food on flat plates. With his long, thin beak, the stork couldn't eat anything at all.

"Oh dear, aren't you hungry?" asked the fox. Without waiting for a reply, he said, "Well, I suppose if you won't eat your dinner, I'll have to." And he ate all of the stork's dinner as well as his own.

The stork was angry at the way the fox had tricked him, and he thought of a clever way to get his revenge. The following week, the stork invited the fox to dine at *his* home.

When the fox arrived, he was so hungry that his mouth was watering. But when he sat down at the table, he saw that the stork had put all the food into jugs with long, narrow necks.

The stork had no trouble getting at the food with his long, slender beak, but the fox couldn't reach any of it. This time, he had to watch as the stork ate both dinners!

MORAL: *If you play tricks on people, they might do the same to you.*

THE DOG
IN THE MANGER

One day, a dog was wandering through the countryside. He hadn't eaten for a whole day, and he was very hungry.

When he came to a farm, the dog went into the stable. "Perhaps I will find some food in here," he thought.

But all the dog found was a manger filled with hay. "Well," he thought, "I can't eat this, but at least it will make a nice, warm bed." And he jumped into the manger and went to sleep.

Sometime later, the dog felt something soft nuzzling him. It was the nose of one of the horses who lived in the stable. He was standing over the manger, and another horse was behind him.

"Sorry to disturb you," said the horse, "but we'd like our dinner now. Would you please get out of the manger so that we can eat our hay?"

"Now go away!"

"No, I will not!" barked the dog.

"Why?" asked the surprised horse. "You can't eat this hay, can you?"

"No, of course not," said the dog.

"Then why not let us have it?" asked the horse.

"Because if I can't eat, I don't want anyone else to eat, either!" said the dog. "Now go away!"

So the poor horses went hungry, all because of a selfish dog.

MORAL: *Don't keep others from having what you can't use.*

THE TOWN MOUSE AND
THE COUNTRY MOUSE

Once there was a little mouse who lived in the country. He had a cozy little nest under a tree, and plenty of seeds and berries to eat. He was a very happy mouse.

One day, his cousin from town came to visit him. Country Mouse gave his cousin a delicious meal of acorns and black currants. Then he made up a warm bed of leaves and straw for him.

But Town Mouse thought the acorns were tough and the black currants sour. The bed felt hard and scratchy.

"Life in the country is no fun at all," said Town Mouse the next day. "Come to town with me, Cousin, and I'll show you how exciting life can be!"

So the two mice left for town. They walked all day, until they came to a big, fine house. "Here we are at last," said Town Mouse.

They crept into the house, and Town Mouse took his cousin straight to the dining room. There they found a table laid with bowls of fruit, platters of cheese and biscuits, and trays of chocolates and cakes. It all looked delicious!

"I told you life in town was exciting!" said Town Mouse. The two mice scampered up onto the table and began to eat.

Suddenly the door opened, and a woman walked into the room.

"Eek! Mice!" she shrieked, swatting at the table with a cloth.

The mice were terrified. They ran from the table as quickly as they could.

"Follow me!" called Town Mouse, and he led his cousin to a dark little hole in the wall. Country Mouse's heart was beating like a drum.

The mice stayed there in the dark until everything seemed quiet again. Then Town Mouse peeped out.

"It's safe," he said to Country Mouse. "Let's go."

A big black-and-white cat chased the mice

But as soon as the mice had crept out of the hole, a big black-and-white cat ran into the room. He chased the mice all around the dining room until they managed to escape through a crack between the floorboards. They stayed under the floorboards all night.

The next morning, Country Mouse told his cousin, "Thank you for showing me your home, but I don't think I'll stay any longer. I'm going back to the country, where I can be safe and happy!"

MORAL: *A safe and simple life is better than an exciting but dangerous one.*